THE WHALES' SONG

To Isha D.S.

To Lin G.B.

A Red Fox Book

Published by Random House Children's Books
20 Vauxhall Bridge Road, London SW1V 2SA

A division of Random House UK Ltd
London Melbourne Sydney Auckland
Johannesburg and agencies throughout the world

First published by Hutchinson Children's Books 1990

Red Fox edition 1993
Reprinted 1993, 1994 (twice)

© *Text Dyan Sheldon 1990*
© *Illustrations Gary Blythe 1990*

Printed in China

RANDOM HOUSE UK Limited Reg. No. 954009

ISBN 0 09 973760 4

THE WHALES' SONG

Story by Dyan Sheldon

Illustrations by Gary Blythe

RED FOX

*L*ILLY'S *grandmother told her a story.*

'Once upon a time,' she said, 'the ocean was filled with whales. They were as big as the hills. They were as peaceful as the moon. They were the most wondrous creatures you could ever imagine.'

*L*ILLY climbed on to her grandmother's lap.

'I used to sit at the end of the jetty and listen for whales,' said Lilly's grandmother. 'Sometimes I'd sit there all day and all night. Then all of a sudden I'd see them coming from miles away. They moved through the water as if they were dancing.'

'*B*UT how did they
know you were there,
Grandma?' asked Lilly.
'How would they find
you?'

Lilly's grandmother
smiled. 'Oh, you had to
bring them something
special. A perfect shell.
Or a beautiful stone. And
if they liked you the
whales would take your
gift and give you
something in return.'

'WHAT would they give you, Grandma?' asked Lilly. 'What did you get from the whales?'

Lilly's grandmother sighed. 'Once or twice,' she whispered, 'once or twice I heard them sing.'

*L*ILLY's uncle Frederick stomped into the room. 'You're nothing but a daft old fool!' he snapped. 'Whales were important for their meat, and for their bones, and for their blubber. If you have to tell Lilly something, then tell her something useful. Don't fill her head with nonsense. Singing whales indeed!'

'*T*HERE were whales here millions of years before there were ships, or cities, or even cavemen,' continued Lilly's grandmother. 'People used to say they were magical.'

'People used to eat them and boil them down for oil!' grumbled Lilly's uncle Frederick. And he turned his back and stomped out to the garden.

*L*ILLY dreamt about whales.

In her dreams she saw them, as large as mountains and bluer than the sky. In her dreams she heard them singing, their voices like the wind. In her dreams they leapt from the water and called her name.

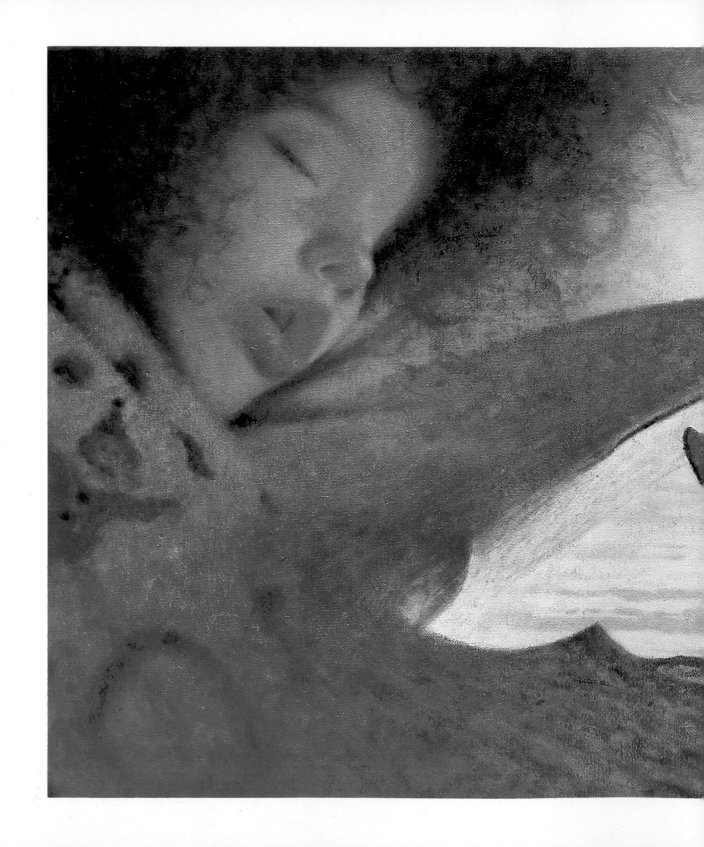

*N*ext morning Lilly
went down to the ocean.
She went where no one
fished or swam or sailed
their boats. She walked
to the end of the old
jetty, the water was empty
and still. Out of her
pocket she took a yellow
flower and dropped it in
the water.

'This is for you,' she
called into the air.

*L*ILLY sat at the end
of the jetty and waited.

She waited all morning
and all afternoon.

Then, as dusk began to
fall, Uncle Frederick
came down the hill after
her. 'Enough of this
foolishness,' he said.
'Come on home. I'll not
have you dreaming your
life away.'

*T*HAT night, Lilly awoke suddenly.

The room was bright with moonlight. She sat up and listened. The house was quiet. Lilly climbed out of bed and went to the window. She could hear something in the distance, on the far side of the hill.

*S*HE *raced outside
and down to the shore.
Her heart was pounding
as she reached the sea.*

*There enormous in the
ocean, were the whales.*

*They leapt and jumped
and spun across the moon.*

*Their singing filled up
the night.*

*Lilly saw her yellow
flower dancing on the
spray.*

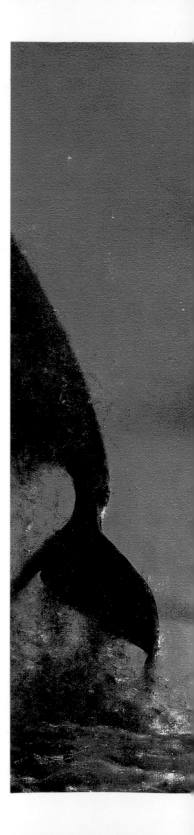

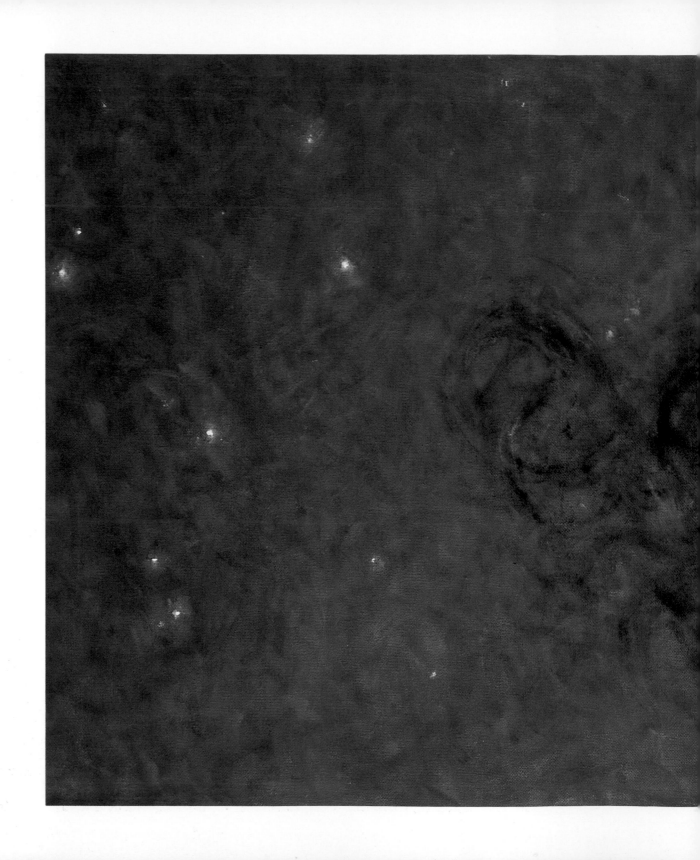

*M*INUTES *passed, or maybe hours. Suddenly Lilly felt the breeze rustle her nightdress and the cold nip at her toes. She shivered and rubbed her eyes. Then it seemed the ocean was still again and the night black and silent.*

Lilly thought she must have been dreaming. She stood up and turned for home. Then from far, far away, on the breath of the wind she heard,

'Lilly!
Lilly!'
The whales were calling her name.

Some bestselling Red Fox picture books

THE BIG ALFIE AND ANNIE ROSE STORYBOOK
by Shirley Hughes
OLD BEAR
by Jane Hissey
OI! GET OFF OUR TRAIN
by John Burningham
DON'T DO THAT!
by Tony Ross
NOT NOW, BERNARD
by David McKee
ALL JOIN IN
by Quentin Blake
THE WHALES' SONG
by Gary Blythe and Dyan Sheldon
JESUS' CHRISTMAS PARTY
by Nicholas Allan
THE PATCHWORK CAT
by Nicola Bayley and William Mayne
MATILDA
by Hilaire Belloc and Posy Simmonds
WILLY AND HUGH
by Anthony Browne
THE WINTER HEDGEHOG
by Ann and Reg Cartwright
A DARK, DARK TALE
by Ruth Brown
HARRY, THE DIRTY DOG
by Gene Zion and Margaret Bloy Graham
DR XARGLE'S BOOK OF EARTHLETS
by Jeanne Willis and Tony Ross
WHERE'S THE BABY?
by Pat Hutchins